TIPS FOR GOING GREEN

TIPS FOR GOING GREEN

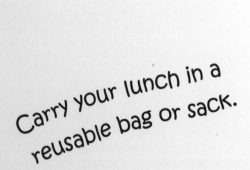

Turn off the light when you leave a room.

Eat less meat.

Walk or ride your bike when you can.

Encourage your friends to go green!

Pick up litter.

Take shorter showers.

Don't let water run while you brush your teeth.

Carry your lunch in a reusable bag or sack.

Miss Fox's Class GOES GREEN

Eileen Spinelli

Illustrated by Anne Kennedy

Albert Whitman & Company, Chicago, Illinois

Library of Congress Cataloging-in-Publication Data

Spinelli, Eileen.
Miss Fox's class goes green / Eileen Spinelli ; illustrated by Anne Kennedy.
p. cm.
Summary: The students in Miss Fox's class lead their school in making choices to help keep
the planet healthy, such as turning off lights when leaving a room, taking shorter showers,
and using cloth bags instead of plastic ones.
ISBN 978-0-8075-5166-0
[1. Environmental protection—Fiction. 2. Green movement—Fiction. 3. Schools—Fiction.
4. Animals—Fiction.] I. Kennedy, Anne, 1955- ill. II. Title.
PZ7.S7566Mi 2009   [E]—dc22

The illustrations were done in watercolors, ink, and dyes.
The design is by Carol Gildar.

For more information about Albert Whitman & Company,
please visit our web site at www.albertwhitman.com.

To Paul and Mary Margaret Rode.—E.S.

For Jack, who draws a good squirrel.—A.K.

The morning Miss Fox came to school on a bicycle, her students were surprised.

"Does your car have a flat tire?" asked Mouse.

"No," said Miss Fox. "But cars pollute the air. I've decided to drive only when I must. I am going green."

"You don't look sick to me," said Raccoon.

Miss Fox chuckled. "Going green isn't about being sick. It's about keeping our earth healthy. Who will help?"

Everyone piped up: "ME!"

"Wonderful!" said Miss Fox. And then she wrote three things on the blackboard.

1. Use less stuff — recycle.
2. Use less energy.
3. Use less water.

"Can you do it?" asked Miss Fox.
"We can do it!" the students replied.
Miss Fox pumped her fist. "Yes—we're going green!"

Frog jumped up. "I can use less water." He grinned.
"I can stop taking showers."

Bunny pinched her nose. "You will get very stinky."

Miss Fox said, "Frog doesn't have to stop taking showers.
He can just take shorter ones."

Squirrel called out, "I know how to save paper. No more homework!"

Miss Fox smiled. "That's not going to happen. But you can use both sides of the paper."

Mouse said, "Turn off the lights when we leave a room."

Bear had an idea, too. "Sharpen old crayons."

"Now you're talking!" said Miss Fox.

That night Mouse stepped into the shower. She liked long sudsy showers. With lots of singing.

But Mouse was going green. So she took a short shower and sang afterwards.

Raccoon was getting ready for bed. "Brrr," she said. "It's chilly." She thought of asking her mom to turn up the heat. But Raccoon wanted to be green. So she took an extra blanket from the shelf.

When Squirrel saw Super-flash Bubble-soled Buzzard sneakers in Barney's Shoe Shop, he told his sister, "I want those!"

But Squirrel was green now, so he had second thoughts. "There is still a lot of fun-and-run in my old sneakers."

Bunny went to the supermarket with her dad. When her dad started packing groceries in a plastic bag, Bunny said, "It takes mucho years for one plastic bag to decompose."

The next time Bunny and her dad went shopping, they brought along a bag made of cloth.

On Saturday Young Bear was watching TV. His friend Possum stopped by. "Do you want to play ball?" he asked.

Young Bear grabbed his glove and ran out the door.
He was halfway down the street when he remembered
something. "I forgot to turn off the TV!"

"So what?" said Possum.

"So—I'm going green," said Young Bear. "Wait just a minute.
I'll be right back. I'll turn off the light, too."

Frog went to visit Uncle Toad. Uncle Toad had a scooter in his shed. He was giving it to Frog. Frog couldn't wait to ride that scooter!

But Uncle Toad also had old jars and newspapers in his shed. And Frog wanted to be green.

"I can help you load these into your truck," said Frog. "We can take them to the recycling center. I can ride the scooter later."

At school the next day, Miss Fox's class held a toy swap.
"I'm tired of my sparkle yo-yo," said Bunny.
"I'll trade you my umbrella hat," said Raccoon.

"Who wants my T-Rex mask?" asked Squirrel.
"I'll take that," said Frog. "Here's my talking tomato."

Day after day, Miss Fox's class made good green choices.
They picked up litter from the schoolyard without being told.

They planted a tree in honor of Miss Fox's birthday.

One morning the principal showed up at school on a bicycle.
"Look!" Bunny called. "Mr. Moose is going green, too!"
The students cheered.

The next day Miss Fox's class had lots of company going green.

Now it was . . .

the whole school!

TIPS FOR GOING **GREEN**

Carry your own cloth bag to the supermarket.

Share rides or take the train or bus.

Turn off computers and other appliances when you're not using them.

Recycle newspapers, cans, plastic, and bottles.

Use fluorescent light bulbs.

Wash your clothes in cold water.

Plant a tree.